A Note to Parents and Caregivers:

Read-it! Readers are for children who are just starting on the amazing road to reading. These beautiful books support both the acquisition of reading skills and the love of books.

The RED LEVEL presents familiar topics using common words and repeating sentence patterns.
The BLUE LEVEL presents new ideas using a larger vocabulary and varied sentence structure.
The YELLOW LEVEL presents more challenging ideas, a broad vocabulary, and wide variety in sentence structure.

When sharing a book with your child, read in short stretches, pausing often to talk about the pictures. Have your child turn the pages and point to the pictures and familiar words. And be sure to reread favorite stories or parts of stories.

There is no right or wrong way to share books with children. Find time to read with your child and pass on the legacy of literacy.

Adria F. Klein, Ph.D.
Professor Emeritus
California State University
San Bernardino, California

First American edition published in 2003 by
Picture Window Books
5115 Excelsior Boulevard
Suite 232
Minneapolis, MN 55416
1-877-845-8392
www.picturewindowbooks.com

First published in Great Britain by Franklin Watts, 96 Leonard Street, London, EC2A 4XD
Text © Maggie Moore 2001
Illustration © Steve Cox 2001

Printed in the United States of America.
1 2 3 4 5 6 08 07 06 05 04 03

Library of Congress Cataloging-in-Publication Data
Moore, Maggie.
  Jack and the beanstalk / by Maggie Moore ; illustrated by Steve Cox.—1st American
ed.
    p. cm. — (Read-it! Fairy tale readers)
  Summary: A boy climbs to the top of a huge beanstalk, where he uses his quick wits
to outsmart a giant and make his and his mother's fortune.
  ISBN 1-4048-0059-X
  [1. Fairy tales. 2. Giants—Folklore. 3. Folklore—England.] I. Cox, Steve, ill. II. Title.
III. Series.
  PZ8.M8038 Jac 2003
  398.2'0942'02—dc21
      [E]   2002072297

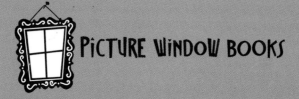

PiCTURE WiNDOW BOOKS

Jack and the Beanstalk

Written by Maggie Moore

Illustrated by Steve Cox

Reading Advisors:
Adria F. Klein, Ph.D.
Professor Emeritus, California State University
San Bernardino, California

Ruth Thomas
Durham Public Schools
Durham, North Carolina

R. Ernice Bookout
Durham Public Schools
Durham, North Carolina

Picture Window Books
Minneapolis, Minnesota

Once upon a time there
was a boy called Jack.

Jack and his mother were very poor. All they had was a cow.

So, one day, Jack went to the market to sell the cow.

On the way, Jack met a little old man who wanted to buy the cow.

"I'll give you five magic beans," he told Jack.

When Jack got home,
he gave the magic beans
to his mother.

Jack's mother was very angry. She threw the beans out of the window.

During the night, the magic beans grew and grew.

By morning, a beanstalk
reached high into the sky.

Jack decided to climb the beanstalk. He climbed and climbed, and when he reached the top, he found

a huge castle!

Jack went inside.

Suddenly, the floor began to shake, and Jack heard a very loud voice.

16

"Fee, fi, fo, fum, I smell the blood of an Englishman!"

"Be he alive or be he dead, I'll grind his bones to make my bread!"

It was a giant! Jack ran
into a cupboard to hide.

The giant sat down and ate a huge meal of five sheep.

Then he called for his hen.
Jack watched as the hen
laid a perfect golden egg.

The giant was full after his meal and fell fast asleep.

So, Jack came out of the cupboard and quickly picked up the giant's hen.

But the hen began to
squawk and flap its wings.
The giant woke up!

"Fee, fi, fo, fum, I smell the blood of an Englishman!" he shouted.

Jack ran back to the beanstalk and climbed down as fast as he could.

"I'll get you!" yelled the giant as he chased Jack.

27

Jack reached the bottom,
picked up his ax, and
chopped down the beanstalk.

The giant fell to the ground
with a thud.

That was the end of him!

The hen laid a golden egg
every day,

and Jack and his mother
were never poor again.

Red Level

The Best Snowman, by Margaret Nash 1-4048-0048-4
Bill's Baggy Pants, by Susan Gates 1-4048-0050-6
Cleo and Leo, by Anne Cassidy 1-4048-0049-2
Felix on the Move, by Maeve Friel 1-4048-0055-7
Jasper and Jess, by Anne Cassidy 1-4048-0061-1
The Lazy Scarecrow, by Jillian Powell 1-4048-0062-X
Little Joe's Big Race, by Andy Blackford 1-4048-0063-8
The Little Star, by Deborah Nash 1-4048-0065-4
The Naughty Puppy, by Jillian Powell 1-4048-0067-0
Selfish Sophie, by Damian Kelleher 1-4048-0069-7

Blue Level

The Bossy Rooster, by Margaret Nash 1-4048-0051-4
Jack's Party, by Ann Bryant 1-4048-0060-3
Little Red Riding Hood, by Maggie Moore 1-4048-0064-6
Recycled!, by Jillian Powell 1-4048-0068-9
The Sassy Monkey, by Anne Cassidy 1-4048-0058-1
The Three Little Pigs, by Maggie Moore 1-4048-0071-9

Yellow Level

Cinderella, by Barrie Wade 1-4048-0052-2
The Crying Princess, by Anne Cassidy 1-4048-0053-0
Eight Enormous Elephants, by Penny Dolan 1-4048-0054-9
Freddie's Fears, by Hilary Robinson 1-4048-0056-5
Goldilocks and the Three Bears, by Barrie Wade 1-4048-0057-3
Mary and the Fairy, by Penny Dolan 1-4048-0066-2
Jack and the Beanstalk, by Maggie Moore 1-4048-0059-X
The Three Billy Goats Gruff, by Barrie Wade 1-4048-0070-0